SUPERTATO

BUBBLY TROUBLY!

Meet Sue and Paul:

Sue Hendra and **Paul Linnet** have been making books together
since 2009 when they came up with *Barry the Fish with Fingers*,
and since then they haven't stopped. If you've ever wondered
which one does the writing and which does the illustrating,
wonder no more . . . they both do both!

To our lovely friend Dr. Stu

SIMON & SCHUSTER

First published in Great Britain in 2021 by Simon & Schuster UK Ltd • 1st Floor, 222 Gray's Inn Road, London, WC1X 8HB
Text and illustrations copyright © 2021 Sue Hendra and Paul Linnet
The right of Sue Hendra and Paul Linnet to be identified as the authors and illustrators of this work
has been asserted by them in accordance with the Copyright, Designs and Patents Act, 1988
A CIP catalogue record for this book is available from the British Library upon request
978-1-4711-8921-0 (PB) • 978-1-4711-8922-7 (eBook) • Printed in China • 10 9 8 7 6 5 4 3 2 1

SUPERTATO
BUBBLY TROUBLY!

SUE HENDRA
PAUL LINNET

SIMON & SCHUSTER
London   New York   Sydney   Toronto   New Delhi

It was night-time in the supermarket
and the veggies were enjoying their weekly bath.

"Look, Supertato, a bubble hat!" said Cucumber.

"I've got a bubbly beard,"
said Aubergine.

"I've made a bubble cave,"
said Carrot.

"Look what I've made," said Tomato. "It's a Bubble-A-Saurus!"

"Wow!" said Cucumber. "We need more bubbles. Quick, someone pass the bubble mixture!"

"Allow me," sniggered The Evil Pea, swapping the Bubbly Bubbles for . . .

TROUBLY

BUBBLES!

There were already a LOT of bubbles,

but soon,
the bubbles doubled!

"That's the last I'll see of those veggie nitwits for a while," cackled the Pea.

"Oooo, what's this? I've got their Duckie!
Mwah ha ha ha ha!"

Trapped down in the bubbles,
it was very confusing.

"We didn't want to double the bubbles!" cried Cucumber.
"I can't see!" sobbed Tomato.
"I don't know where I am!" called Carrot.

Then somebody spoke.

"RELAX MAN,
EVERYONE COOL IT."

"I know that voice," said Supertato.
"It's Mystic Mango!
Do you know where
we are?"

"YOU'RE IN THE CHILLED AISLE, SUPER DUDE!

LOOK, VEGGIES, DON'T PANIC.
YOU CAN SORT OUT THIS MESS.
THE SOLUTION IS HERE
SO GET LOOKING! DON'T STRESS."

The solution is here? Hmmm . . .
thought Supertato.
First, they tried the
bubbly biscuit aisle . . .
But all they found
were bubbles.

It was the same in the bubbly
baking aisle . . .

Then all of a sudden,
Tomato spotted something . . .

"Nobody move!" he shouted.
"We're in the stationery aisle."

"The solution must be pencils! Mystic Mango means we should pop the bubbles with the pointy pencils!"

So Tomato set to work. POP ... POP ...

POP ...

"This is going to take quite a long time, Supertato."

"NO, NO, GROOVY VEGGIES, DON'T BOTHER WITH THOSE. WHAT YOU SEEK CLEANS YOU UP FROM YOUR HEAD TO YOUR TOES!"

"I know what it is," shouted Cucumber. "It's a flannel! We can WIPE the bubbles away!"

But Cucumber tried,
and it didn't work.

"The flannel just moves them
around, Supertato!

It's not a flannel
is it, Mystic Mango?"
said Cucumber.

"SORRY, MAN. IT SURE
WAS A GROOVY SUGGESTION,
BUT NO.

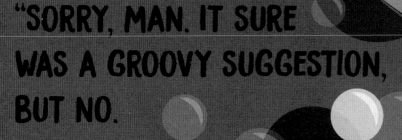

RELAX, VEGGIE DUDES.
THE ANSWER IS NEAR.
FIND A MAGICAL CASTLE
AND THE BUBBLES WILL CLEAR . . ."

"Where are we going to find a magical castle?" said Supertato.

"Is that one?" asked Carrot.

"It certainly looks like one!" cried the veggies.

But as they got closer, they realised it wasn't a magical castle at all.

"It's just lots of bars of soap!" said the veggies, disappointed.

But Supertato wasn't disappointed . . .

"OF COURSE!
How could I forget?"

"Is this the end for the bubbles?" said one Pineapple to another.

"You bet it is, Pineapples! Soap makes bubbles disappear.

Don't believe me? Maybe **you** should try it!"

"Time to get popping!"

Soon, almost all the bubbles were gone.

"Oooops, looks like we've missed some," said Tomato.
"And what's that behind them?"

"Come on, little Duckie, it's a lovely day for a . . .

Uh-oh!"

"**Supertato**, thanks to you all the bubbles have disappeared!"

"Not **ALL** the bubbles, Tomato!

I've saved just one . . ."

The veggies were thrilled.
"Supertato, we LOVE you!"

"Supertato, you're **amazing!**"

"Supertato, I'm your **biggest** fan!"

"Oh no you're not, Tomato . . .

. . . THIS is my BIGGEST fan!

And it's going to blow that pea over to the freezy aisle where he belongs.

Fishfingers, would you mind POPPING
that pea back in the freezer for me, please?"

"Oh yes, Supertato.

We'd be delighted!"

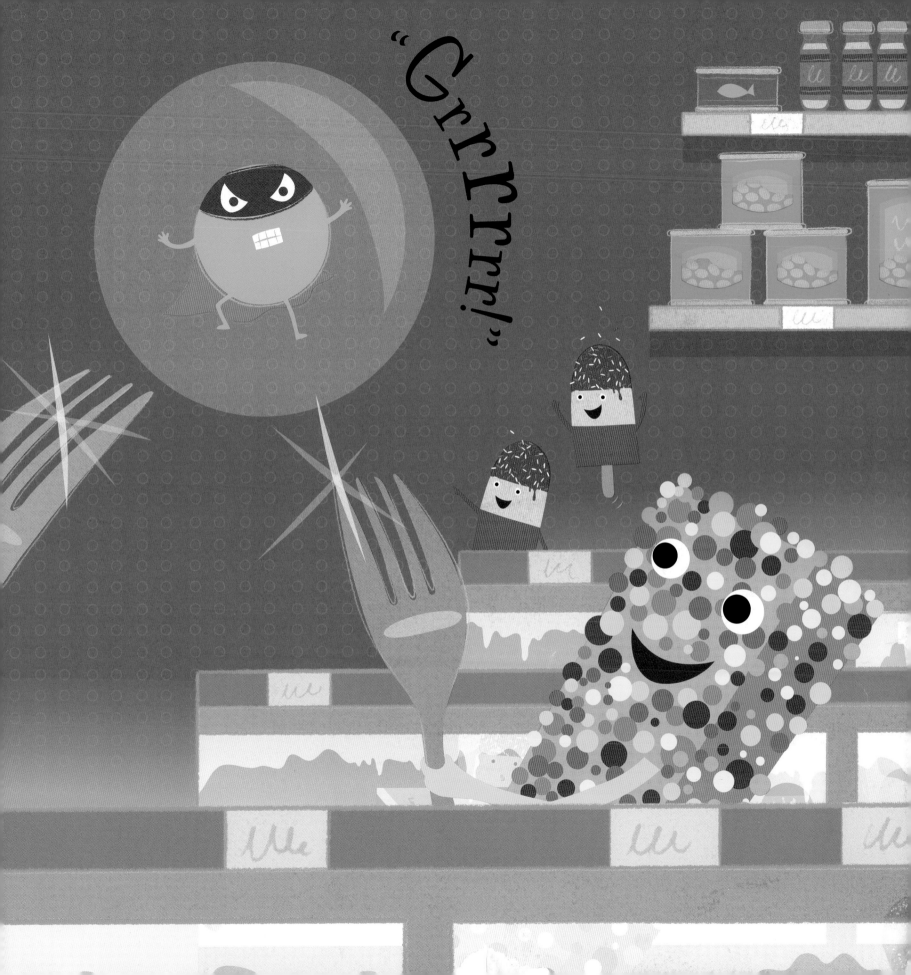

"Grrrrrr!"

If you like

SUPERTATO

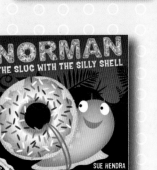

BUBBLY TROUBLY!

you'll love these other

adventures from

SUE HENDRA & PAUL LINNET

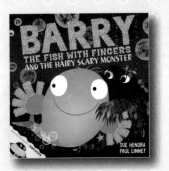